There are 6 books in all which will take your child from age 3 until Primary One. Younger children won't necessarily understand all the stories. That's fine, they don't have to. Learning to **HOLD HANDS** and **WAIT** are the key points, the rest will come in time.

It's never too early for a child to get into good road safety habits that will last them a lifetime. So make sure they're following the best possible example and Go Safe every time you cross.

All that's left to say is – enjoy!

The books support Curriculum for Excellence.

Children can follow Ziggy's adventures online at: **www.gosafewithziggy.com**

D1422216

Shout
'Zab-a-Ding-a-Doo'
to Ziggy!

It's time for him to go back
to his own planet.

So let's make sure
he knows how to
Go Safe.

It's only a few days until
the start of the
new school term.

Maggie and Ziggy can't wait to start school.

Maggie is going to be
a big Primary One.

And Ziggy's going to be a big
Nanoo-Nee-Nee-Na-Na.

That's what they call Primary One
on Ziggy's planet, you see.

I wonder what they call
Primary Two?

There's still a **lot to do**
before school starts.

**'We'd better make
a list to take to the shops,'**
says Mum and spreads
a big piece of paper
on the table.

a lunchbox

a pencil case

Things Maggie still
needs for school —

white socks

black shoes

**Can you remember
all the things
you need for
starting school?**

It's time to go shopping.

Andrew, Maggie and Ziggy climb into their car-seats.

Ziggy is really going to miss his special seat.

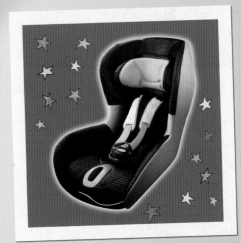

He takes a picture with his magic watch so that he can show his friends back home. They won't believe that all the kids on Earth get their own special car seat.

Lucky things.

Mum straps everyone
in securely with
their seatbelts.

**'There's a lot of
traffic today,'** says Ziggy.

'Traffic,' smiles Mum.
'Great word, Ziggy.'

**'When I first came here
I didn't even know
what traffic was,'**
smiles Ziggy proudly.

'I've always known about traffic,' says Maggie.

'Traffic is cars and buses and lorries and vans and trucks and more lorries and... and well I probably knew what traffic was before I was even born.'

'Maggie knew what *everything* was before she was born,'

Andrew says, giving Ziggy a nudge.

Mum stops at a red traffic light.

Jasmine and her Daddy
  are standing with their bikes,
waiting to cross the road.

**'They're waiting for
the green man
to come on,'**

smiles Ziggy.

The shopping centre is really busy and everyone **cheers** when Mum eventually finds a parking space.

Andrew, Maggie and Ziggy wait until Mum comes round to open the door for them.

'Now what do we have to remember about car parks?' asks Mum.

'That it takes ages to find a parking space,' mutters Maggie cheekily.

'Car parks are just funny shaped roads,' says Ziggy.

'So we always have to hold hands and keep looking and listening for cars.'

'That's right,' says Mum.

'I knew that,' says Maggie. 'I am nearly in Primary One, you know.'

The shopping centre
is huge.

Ziggy likes the supermarket.

But the best bit of all
is the row upon row of big,
fat juicy **cabbages.**

Ziggy wishes he could jump
in and gobble them all up.

Yummeeeeeee eeeeeeeeeeeeeee eeeeeeeeeeeee.

It's the **first day** of term.

Andrew and Maggie
both look very smart
in their school uniforms.

The family walk to school together.
Ziggy can't believe that this
time tomorrow he'll be
starting school too.

Zab-a-Ding-a-Doo!

Ziggy and Maggie help
Mum and Andrew find
a safe place to cross.

'This is a good place to cross,'
says Maggie,
**'because we can see the traffic
coming and the traffic can see us.'**

**'And we have to use
our ears too,'** says Ziggy,
**'to make sure we can hear
the traffic coming.'**

'My two wee geniuses,'
laughs Mum.

**'Now stay well back from
the kerb and hold hands
until it's safe to cross.'**

'I think kerbs are really clever,'
says Ziggy, taking a picture with his magic watch.

'You do?' says Maggie,
thinking that sometimes Ziggy is
quite a strange little alien indeed.

'Kerbs are like the pavement's way of
saying STOP without having to write
stop all the way along the edge of the road.'

Ziggy zaps his watch again and this time it projects
the word STOP all along the pavement.

Andrew gasps. 'You're right Ziggy.
It would take someone a zillion years to write
stop on the side of every road.'

'And how silly would it be to do that?'
says Maggie.

'Primary Ones can't even read yet.'

Everyone **looks** up and down the road to **check** that there's no traffic coming.
Then they check **again.**
The road is clear so it's safe to cross.

And what do we always have to do when we cross the road?

'Hold hands!

'Look for traffic!'

'And Listen for traffic!'

Ziggy gives Maggie
and Andrew a big kiss
at the school gate.

**'Have a Zab-a-Ding-a-Doo
first day, Maggie!'**
says Ziggy.

**'And you have a
Dab-a-Fingy-Doo
last day!'** says Maggie,
not getting it quite right.

'I'll try,' mumbles
Ziggy with a lump
in his throat.

He's going to miss his
Earth family so much.

Ziggy takes Mum's hand
and they head home.

**'That was very clever
what you said about kerbs
this morning,'** says Mum
trying to cheer Ziggy up,
**'that kerbs tell us to stop
without any words.'**

Ziggy smiles and thinks
for a moment.
**'Like a cuddle says I love you
without any words?'**

'Just like that,' says Mum
and cuddles Ziggy tightly.

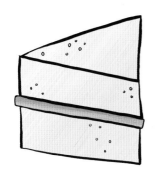

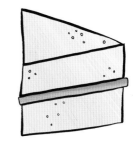

Mum has organized a **tea party**
after school for Ziggy.

Andrew, Maggie and **Jasmine**
are enjoying tucking into cheese sandwiches
and Granny Walker's special crispie cakes.

And Ziggy is enjoying tucking into
cabbage sandwiches and cabbage cakes.

Yum, yum, yum, yum, yum!

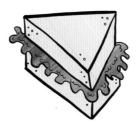

Mum tells everyone to gather round and hands Ziggy an enormous box with a huge bow.

'**We're going to really miss you Ziggy,**'
says Maggie wiping a big tear from her eye.

'**Me too,**' said Ziggy. '**But I've been working on
a surprise of my own. I phoned my Daddy earlier
and he's set up a website for me, so we can
play games together and keep in-touch.**'

'**Zab-a-Ding-a-Doo!**' shrieks Maggie.

'**I think you've learned everything you need
to know now Ziggy,**' says Mum squeezing Ziggy tightly.

'**And Maggie's learned something very,
very important too,**' says Ziggy very seriously.

'**Oh,**' says Mum. '**What's that?**'

Ziggy roars with laughter.

'**How to say Zab-a-Ding-a-Doo!**'

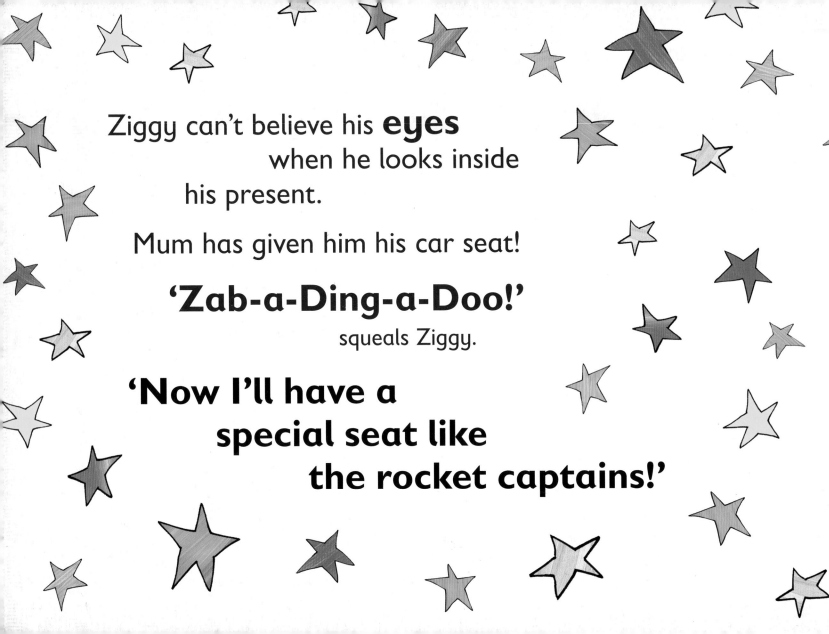

Ziggy can't believe his **eyes** when he looks inside his present.

Mum has given him his car seat!

'Zab-a-Ding-a-Doo!'
squeals Ziggy.

'Now I'll have a special seat like the rocket captains!'

'Zab-a-Ding-a-Doo,'
waves Ziggy as he gets
ready to go into his rocket.

**'Remember to Go Safe
every time you cross!'**

'We will,' chorus the kids.

And we'll Go Safe too, Ziggy.

Zab-a-Ding-a-Doo!

You can look and listen to all the books in the Ziggy series by visiting
www.gosafewithziggy.com

What you should know about crossing the road with pre-school children

Just talking about **stop**, **look** and **listen** isn't enough.

Young children find it difficult to stop and will be too easily distracted to properly look and listen for traffic.

Children aren't ready to cross a road by themselves until they are at least **8 years of age**.

Real learning comes from real experiences.

Every time you cross a road with a young child, the child will learn from **what you do and what you say.**

Every time.

If you take risks when crossing the road, the child with you **won't** learn to Go Safe.